gluttony

Christian,

Hope you're having time
for a little gluttony as you
recover! Best,
Jon & Grit

gluttony

*Ample Tales of
Epicurean Excess*

EDITED BY JOHN MILLER
AND BENEDICT COSGROVE

CHRONICLE BOOKS
SAN FRANCISCO

Page 136 constitutes a continuation of the copyright page.
To maintain the authentic style of each writer included herein, quirks
of spelling and grammar remain unchanged from their original state.

Printed in the United States of America.

Library of Congress Cataloging-in-Publication Data:
Gluttony: ample tales of epicurean excess / edited by John Miller
and Benedict Cosgrove.
p.   cm.
ISBN 0-8118-1269-3
1. Gluttony—Literary collections. I. Miller, John, 1959– .
II. Cosgrove, Benedict.
PN6071.G55G55 1996
808.8'0353—dc20
96-2646
CIP

Editing and design: Big Fish Books
Composition: Eleanor A. Reagh, Big Fish Books

Distributed in Canada by Raincoast Books,
8680 Cambie Street, Vancouver, B.C. V6P 6M9

10 9 8 7 6 5 4 3 2 1

Chronicle Books
275 Fifth Street
San Francisco, CA 94103

"Pecat de gola Deu el persona"

["God pardons the sin of gluttony"]*

—Ancient Catalan Proverb

Thanks K — JM

Thanks Max — BC

CONTENTS

M.F.K. FISHER

G is for Gluttony

T IS A curious fact that no man likes to call himself a glutton, and yet each of us has in him a trace of gluttony, potential or actual. I cannot believe that there exists a single coherent human being who will not confess, at least to himself, that once or twice he has stuffed himself to the bursting point, on anything from quail financière to flapjacks, for no other reason than the beastlike satisfaction of his belly. In fact I pity anyone who has not permitted himself this sensual experience, if only to determine what his own private limitations are, and where, for himself alone, gourmandism ends and gluttony begins.

It is different for each of us, and the size of a man's paunch has little to do with the kind of appetite which fills it. Diamond Jim Brady, for instance, is more often than not called "the greatest glutton in American history," and so on, simply because he had a really enormous capacity for food. To my mind he was not gluttonous but rather monstrous, in that his stomach was about six times normal size. That he ate at least six times as much as a normal man did not make him a glutton. He was, instead, Gargantuan, in the classical sense. His taste was keen and sure to the time of his death, and that he ate nine portions of sole Marguéry the night George Rector brought the recipe back to New York from Paris especially for him does not mean that he gorged himself upon it but simply that he had room for it.

I myself would like to be able to eat that much of something I really delight in, and I can recognize overtones of envy in the way lesser mortals so easily damned Brady as a glutton, even in the days of excess when he flourished.

Probably this country will never again see so many fat, rich men as were prevalent at the end of the last century, copper kings and railroad millionaires and suchlike literally stuffing themselves to death in imitation of Diamond Jim, whose abnormally large stomach coincided so miraculously with the period. He ate a hundred men like "Betcha-Million" Gates into their oversized coffins simply because he was a historical accident, and it is interesting to speculate on what his influence would be today, when most of the robber barons have gastric ulcers and lunch off crackers and milk at their desks. Certainly it is now unfashionable to overeat in public, and the few

real trenchermen left are careful to practice their gastronomical excesses in the name of various honor-
able and respected food-and-wine societies.

It is safe to say, I think, that never again in our
civilization will gluttony be condoned, much less
socially accepted, as it was at the height of Roman
decadence, when a vomitorium was as necessary a
part of any well-appointed home as a powder room
is today, and throat-ticklers were as common as our
Kleenex. That was, as one almost forgotten writer
has said in an unforgettable phrase, the "period of
insatiable voracity and the peacock's plume," and I
am glad it is far behind me, for I would make but a
weak social figure of a glutton, no matter to what
excesses of hunger I could confess.

My capacity is very limited, fortunately for my
inward as well as outer economy, so that what glut-
tonizing I have indulged in has resulted in bilious-
ness more spiritual than physical. It has, like almost
everyone's in this century, been largely secret. I think

it reached its peak of purely animal satisfaction when I was about seventeen.

I was cloistered then in a school where each avid, yearning young female was allowed to feed at least one of her several kinds of hunger with a daily chocolate bar. I evolved for myself a strangely voluptuous pattern of borrowing, hoarding, begging, and otherwise collecting about seven or eight of these noxious sweets and eating them alone upon a pile of pillows when all the other girls were on the hockey field or some such equally healthful place. If I could eat at the same time a nickel box of soda crackers, brought to me by a stooge among the day girls, my orgiastic pleasure was complete.

I find, in confessing this far-distant sensuality, that even the cool detachment acquired with time does not keep me from feeling both embarrassed and disgusted. What a pig I was!

I am a poor figure of a glutton today in comparison with that frank adolescent cramming. In fact I can think of nothing quite like it in my present make-up. It is true that I overeat at times, through carelessness or a deliberate prolonging of my pleasure in a certain taste, but I do not do it with the voracity of youth. I am probably incapable, really, of such lust. I rather regret it: one more admission of my dwindling powers!

Perhaps the nearest I come to gluttony is with wine. As often as possible, when a really beautiful bottle is before me, I drink all I can of it, even when I know I have had more than I want physically. That is gluttonous.

But I think to myself, when again will I have this taste upon my tongue? Where else in the world is there just such wine as this, with just this bouquet, at just this heat, in just this crystal cup? And when again will I be alive to it as I am this very minute, sitting here on a green hillside above the sea, or here in this dim, murmuring, richly odorous restaurant, or here in this fishermen's café on the wharf? More, more, I think—all of it, to the last exquisite drop, for there is no satiety for me, nor ever has been, in such drinking.

Perhaps this keeps it from being gluttony—not according to the dictionary but in my own lexicon of taste. I do not know.

RUSSELL BAKER

Francs and Beans

S CHANCE WOULD have it, the very evening in 1975 Craig Claiborne ate his historic $4,000 dinner for two with thirty-one dishes and nine wines in Paris, a Lucullan repast for one was prepared and consumed in New York by this correspondent, no slouch himself when it comes to titillating the palate.

Mr. Claiborne won his meal in a television fund-raising auction and had it professionally prepared. Mine was created from spur-of-the-moment inspiration, necessitated when I discovered a note on the stove saying, "Am eating out with Dora and Imogene—make dinner for yourself." It was from the person who regularly does the cooking at my house and, though disconcerted at first, I quickly rose to the challenge.

The meal opened with a 1975 Diet Pepsi served in a disposable bottle. Although its bouquet was negligible, its distinct metallic aftertaste evoked memories of tin cans one had licked experimentally in the first flush of childhood's curiosity.

To create the balance of tastes so cherished by the epicurean palate, I followed with a *pâté de fruites de nuts of Georgia*, prepared according to my own recipe. A half-inch layer of creamy-style peanut butter is troweled onto a graham cracker, then half a banana is crudely diced and pressed firmly into the peanut butter and cemented in place as it were by a second graham cracker.

The accompanying drink was cold milk served in a wide-brimmed jelly glass. This is essential to proper consumption of the pâté, since the entire confection must be dipped into the milk to soften it for eating. In making the presentation to the mouth, one must beware lest the milk-soaked portion of the sandwich fall onto the necktie. Thus, seasoned gourmandisers follow the old maxim of the Breton chefs and "bring the mouth to the jelly glass."

At this point in the meal, the stomach was ready for serious eating, and I prepared beans with bacon grease, a dish I perfected in 1937 while developing my *cuisine du depression.*

The dish is started by placing a pan over very high flame until it becomes dangerously hot. A can of Heinz's pork and beans is then emptied into the pan and allowed to char until it reaches the consistency of hardening concrete. Three strips of bacon are fried to crisps, and when the beans have formed huge dense clots firmly welded to the pan, the bacon grease is poured in and stirred vigorously with a large screwdriver.

This not only adds flavor but also loosens some

of the beans from the side of the pan. Leaving the flame high, I stirred in a three-day-old spaghetti sauce found in the refrigerator, added a sprinkle of chili powder, a large dollop of Major Grey's chutney and a tablespoon of bicarbonate of soda to make the whole dish rise.

Beans with bacon grease is always eaten from the pan with a tablespoon while stand-ing over the kitchen sink. The pan must be thrown away immedi-ately. The correct drink with this dish is a straight shot of room-temperature gin. I had a Gilbey's 1975, which was superb.

For the meat course, I had fried bologna *à la Nutley, Nouveau Jersey*. Six slices of A & P bologna were placed in an ungreased frying pan over maxi-mum heat and held down by a long fork until the entire house filled with smoke. The bologna was turned, fried the same length of time on the other side, then served on air-filled white bread with thick lashings of mayonnaise.

The correct drink for fried bologna *à la Nutley, Nouveau Jersey* is a 1927 Nehi Cola, but since my cellar, alas, had none, I had to make do with a second shot of Gilbey's 1975.

The cheese course was deliciously simple—a single slice of Kraft's individually wrapped yellow sandwich cheese, which was flavored by vigorous rubbing over the bottom of the frying pan to soak up the rich bologna juices. Wine being absolutely *de rigueur* with cheese, I chose a 1974 Muscatel, flavored with a maraschino cherry, and afterwards cleared my palate with three pickled martini onions.

It was time for the fruit. I chose a Del Monte tinned pear, which, regrettably, slipped from the spoon and fell on the floor, necessitating its being blotted with a paper towel to remove cat hairs. To compensate for the resulting loss of pear syrup, I dipped it lightly in hot dog relish which created a unique flavor.

With the pear I drank two shots of Gilbey's 1975 and one shot of Wolfschmidt vodka (nonvintage), the Gilbey's having been exhausted.

At last it was time for the dish the entire meal had been building toward—dessert. With a paring knife, I ripped into a fresh package of Oreos, produced a bowl of My-T-Fine chocolate pudding which had been coagulating in the refrigerator for days and, using a potato masher, crushed a dozen Oreos into the pudding. It was immense.

Between mouthfuls, I sipped a tall, bubbling tumbler of cool Bromo-Seltzer, and finished with six ounces of Maalox. It couldn't have been better.

ANONYMOUS

Moderation in Food

HIS VIRTUE IS too little practised by many who at the same time would be shocked by the charge of excess in drinking. Such is the weakness of human nature, and such the deceitfulness of sin. Yet gluttony is perhaps no less mischievous than drunkenness, and, when properly considered, equally disgraceful. It enfeebles both mind and body, it is a sinful waste, and the frequent forerunner of poverty and want. The victim of this unhappy vice becomes

heavy, idle, and eventually, good for nothing, but to supply a larger feast for the worms of the grave.

The Poet has described persons of this class in the following lines:

> There are a number of us creep
>
> Into this world to eat and sleep;
>
> And know no reason why they're born.
>
> But merely to consume the corn,
>
> Devour the cattle, fowl, and fish,
>
> And leave behind an empty dish.
>
> The crows and ravens do the same,
>
> Unlucky birds of hateful name;
>
> Ravens and crows might fill their place,
>
> And swallow corn and carcases.

The excess, against which we would warn the reader, begins at a point far short of that *brutal* intemperance which shocks every beholder: it begins soon after hunger is appeased, and the animal spirits are refreshed; it begins when the otherwise satiated appetite must be tempted by variety and by dainties; it begins when a person begins to feel oppression.

Listen for a moment to enlightened moralists: "For my part," (says Mr. ADDISON,) "when I behold a fashionable table set out in all its magnificence, I fancy that I see gouts and dropsies, fevers and lethargies, with other innumerable distempers lying in ambuscade among the dishes."

"It has been observed, by medieval writers, that sober excess, in which many indulge by eating and drinking a little too much at every day's dinner, and every night's supper, more effectually undermines the health, than those more rare excesses by which others now and then break in upon a life of general sobriety." Miss HANNAH MORE. It is by no means intended to suggest that extravagance of this sort is confined to the higher ranks of life. Much to be lamented is the fact, that many of the poor have been known to spend more than the day's earnings upon one meal, and in the dearest times have been found the last to practise lessons of frugality. Such persons involve themselves deeply in debt, and sacrifice character and respectability to a fleshly appetite, under the pretext of supporting themselves in their daily labour. The apology is— "We cannot live without it."

Let us consult the physicians.

Dr. CILLYNE: "Most of all the chronical diseases, the infirmities of old age, and the short periods of the lives of Englishmen are owing to repletion." Dr. BUCHAN: "The slave of appetite will ever be the disgrace of human nature. The great rule of diet is to study simplicity. Nature delights in the most plain and simple food; and every animal, except man, follows her dictates. Man alone riots at large and ransacks the whole creation in quest of luxuries to his own destruction." Dr. WILLIAM: "A much greater number of diseases originate upon the whole from irregularities in eating than in drinking."

Hear the word of God. "Be not among wine-bibbers, among riotous eaters of flesh. For the drunkard and the glutton shall come to poverty." (Prov. xxiii. 20, 21.) Jesus, the Son of God, the Saviour of sinners, thus warned his disciples: "Take heed to yourselves lest at any time your hearts be over-charged with surfeiting and drunkenness." (Luke xxi. 34.) Paul, when animating the Christian to a holy warfare, remarks, that "every man who striveth for the mastery is temperate in all things." (I Cor. ix. 25.) And when the Apostles are describing some of the vilest of men, they speak of them as "feeding them-selves without fear—whose God is their belly, whose glory is their shame, whose end is destruction." (Jude 12. Phil. iii. 19.)

If the duty of moderation be obligatory at all times, it derives an additional force from the pressure of public and general affliction in a Season of Scarcity. When multitudes pine at home or abroad, dinnerless every day, economy and temperance are doubly binding: prodigality and gluttony brand their votaries with double infamy and guilt. (See Isa. xxii. 12, 13.) Consider how mean it is to pamper a frail and dying body; how foolish to bring dulness and stupidity over the noble powers of the soul; how ungrateful to abuse the bounty of God; how dreadful to contract a habit so difficult to root up, so apt to grow, and which exposes to the heaviest condemnation! What will *Jesus the Judge* say to the intemperate, the sensualist, the glutton?—

"Debauched souls! that sacrifice
Eternal hopes above the skies,
And pour their lives out all in waste
To the vile idol of their taste!
The highest heaven of their pursuit,
Is to live equal with the brute:
Happy, if they could die as well,
Without a Judge, without a hell.

—WATTS

Is the reader convicted, ashamed, and self condemned? Let him listen to the following affectionate hints. In the first place, repent in deep abasement, humble yourself before God, and intreat him to par-

don you through the mediation of Christ for having abused his bounty, disgraced your rational nature, squandered away precious time and money, which might have been used for nobler purposes, and exhibited a pernicious example to all who have been eye or ear witnesses of your sensuality. Resolve that, by divine assistance, you will put a knife to the throat of this fleshly lust. Be resolute: and in a little time you will attain a command over your appetite that will surprise, and please, and profit you.

But something more is necessary than the sober use of the food which perishes. The *soul* requires richer food, and being immortal, will require it *forever*. Of this food the Saviour speaks, when he says, "My flesh is meat indeed, and my blood is drink indeed: whoso eateth my flesh and drinketh my blood, hath eternal life." By eating the flesh and drinking the blood of Jesus Christ is meant believing on him, and so believing, as to partake of all the spiritual desires which his doctrine tends to excite, and all the spiritual supplies which his grace promises to bestow. Blessed are they who hunger and thirst after such food: it never cloys, it cannot be exhausted, it both strengthens and delights, it detaches from the inordinate love of meaner gratifications, it is the fore-taste of Heaven itself.

Temperance in Pleasure Recommended

Let me particularly exhort youth to temperance in pleasure. Let me admonish them, to be aware of that rock on which thousands, from race to race, continue to split. The love of pleasure, natural to man in every period of his life, glows at this age with excessive ardour. Novelty adds fresh charms, as yet, to every gratification. The world appears to spread a continual feast: and health, vigour, and high spirits, invite them to partake of it without restraint. In vain we warn them of latent dangers. Religion is accused of insufferable severity, of prohibiting enjoyment; and the old, when they offer their admonition, are upbraided with having forgot that they once were young.—And yet, my friends, in what do the constraints of religion, and the counsels of age, with respect to pleasure, amount? They may all be comprised in a few words—not to hurt yourselves, and not to hurt others, by your pursuit of pleasure. Within these bounds, pleasure is lawful; beyond them it becomes criminal, because it is ruinous. Are these restraints any other than what a wise man would choose to impose on himself? We call you not to renounce pleasure, but to enjoy it in safety. Instead of abridging it, we exhort you to pursue it on an extensive plan. We propose measures for securing its possession, and for prolonging its duration.

JOHN KENNEDY TOOLE

A Confederacy of Dunces

ARADISE VENDORS, INCORPORATED, was housed in what had formerly been an automobile repair shop, the dark ground floor of an otherwise unoccupied commercial building on Poydras Street. The garage doors were usually open, giving the passerby an acrid nostrilful of boiling hot dogs and mustard and also of cement soaked over many years by automobile lubricants and motor oils that had dripped and drained from Harmons and Hupmobiles.

The powerful stench of Paradise Vendors, Incorporated, sometimes led the overwhelmed and perplexed stroller to glance through the open door into the darkness of the garage. There his eye fell upon a fleet of large tin hot dogs mounted on bicycle tires. It was hardly an imposing vehicular collection. Several of the mobile hot dogs were badly dented. One crumpled frankfurter lay on its side, its one wheel horizontal above it, a traffic fatality.

Among the afternoon pedestrians who hurried past Paradise Vendors, Incorporated, one formidable figure waddled slowly along. It was Ignatius. Stopping before the narrow garage, he sniffed the fumes from Paradise with great sensory pleasure, the protruding hairs in his nostrils analyzing, cataloging, categorizing, and classifying the distinct odors of hot dog, mustard, and lubricant. Breathing deeply, he wondered whether he also detected the more delicate odor, the fragile scent of hot dog buns. He looked at the white-gloved hands of his Mickey Mouse wristwatch and noticed that he had eaten lunch only an hour before. Still the intriguing aromas were making him salivate actively.

He stepped into the garage and looked around. In a corner an old man was boiling hot dogs in a large institutional pot whose size dwarfed the gas range upon which it rested.

"Pardon me, sir," Ignatius called. "Do you retail here?"

The man's watering eyes turned toward the large visitor.

"What do you want?"

"I would like to buy one of your hot dogs. They smell rather tasty. I was wondering if I could buy just one."

"Sure."

"May I select my own?" Ignatius asked, peering down over the top of the pot. In the boiling water the frankfurters swished and lashed like artificially colored and magnified paramecia. Ignatius filled his lungs with the pungent, sour aroma. "I shall pretend that I am in a smart restaurant and that this is the lobster pond."

"Here, take this fork," the man said, handing Ignatius a bent and corroded semblance of a spear. "Try to keep your hands out of the water. It's like acid. Look what it's done to the fork."

"My," Ignatius said to the old man after having taken his first bite. "These are rather strong. What are the ingredients in these?"

"Rubber, cereal, tripe. Who knows? I wouldn't touch one of them myself."

"They're curiously appealing," Ignatius said, clearing his throat. "I thought that the vibrissae about my nostrils detected something unique while I was outside."

Ignatius chewed with a blissful savagery, studying the scar on the man's nose and listening to his whistling.

"Do I hear a strain from Scarlatti?" Ignatius asked finally.

"I thought I was whistling 'Turkey in the Straw.' "

"I had hoped that you might be familiar with Scarlatti's work. He was the last of the musicians," Ignatius observed and resumed his furious attack upon the long hot dog. "With your apparent musical bent, you might apply yourself to something worthwhile."

Ignatius chewed while the man began his tuneless whistling again. Then he said, "I suspect that you imagine 'Turkey in the Straw' to be a valuable bit of Americana. Well, it is not. It is a discordant abomination."

"I can't see that it matters much."

"It matters a great deal, sir!" Ignatius screamed. "Veneration of such things as 'Turkey in the Straw' is at the very root of our current dilemma."

"Where the hell do you come from? Whadda you want?"

"What is your opinion of a society that considers 'Turkey in the Straw' to be one of the pillars, as it were, of its culture?"

"Who thinks that?" the old man asked worriedly.

"Everyone! Especially folk singers and third-grade teachers. Grimy undergraduates and grammar school-children are always chanting it like sorcerers." Ignatius belched. "I do believe that I shall have another of these savories."

After his fourth hot dog, Ignatius ran his magnificent pink tongue around his lips and up over his moustache and said to the old man, "I cannot recently remember having been so totally satisfied. I was fortunate to find this place. Before me lies a day fraught with God knows what horrors. I am at the moment unemployed and have been launched upon a quest for work. However, I might as well have had the Grail set as my goal. I have been rocketing about the business district for a week now. Apparently I lack some particular perversion which today's employer is seeking."

"No luck, huh?"

"Well, during the week, I have answered only two ads. On some days I am completely enervated by the time I reach Canal Street. On these days I am doing well if I have enough spirit to straggle into a movie palace. Actually, I have seen every film that is playing downtown, and since they are all offensive enough to be held over indefinitely, next week looks particularly bleak."

The old man looked at Ignatius and then at the massive pot, the gas range, and the crumpled carts. He said, "I can hire you right here."

"Thank you very much," Ignatius said condescendingly. "However, I could not work here. This garage is particularly dank, and I'm susceptible to respiratory ailments among a variety of others."

"You wouldn't be working in here, son. I mean as a vendor."

"What?" Ignatius bellowed. "Out in the rain and snow all day long?"

"It don't snow here."

"It has on rare occasions. It probably would again as soon as I trudged out with one of these wagons. I would probably be found in some gutter, icicles dangling from all of my orifices, alley cats pawing over me to draw the warmth from my last breath. No, thank you, sir. I must go. I suspect that I have an appointment of some sort."

Ignatius looked absently at his little watch and saw that it had stopped again.

"Just for a little while," the old man begged. "Try it for a day. How's about it? I need vendors bad."

"A day?" Ignatius repeated disbelievingly. "A day? I can't waste a valuable day. I have places to go and people to see."

"Okay," the old man said firmly. "Then pay me the dollar you owe for them weenies."

"I am afraid that they will all have to be on the house. Or on the garage or whatever it is. My Miss Marple of a mother discovered a number of theater tickets stubs in my pockets last night and has given me only carfare today."

"I'll call in the police."

"Oh, my God!"

"Pay me! Pay me or I'll get the law."

The old man picked up the long fork and deftly placed its two rotting tongs at Ignatius' throat.

"You are puncturing my imported muffler," Ignatius screamed.

"Gimme your carfare."

"I can't walk all the way to Constantinople Street."

"Get a taxi. Somebody at your house can pay the driver when you get there."

"Do you seriously think that my mother will believe me if I tell her that an old man held me up with a fork and took my two nickels?"

"I'm not gonna be robbed again," the old man said, spraying Ignatius with saliva. "That's all that happens to you in the hot dog trade. Hot dog vendors and gas station attendants always get it. Holdups, muggings. Nobody respects a hot dog vendor."

"That is patently untrue, sir. No one respects hot dog vendors more than I. They perform one of our society's few worthwhile services. The robbing of a hot dog vendor is a symbolic act. The theft is not prompted by avarice but rather by a desire to belittle the vendor."

"Shut your goddam fat lip and pay me."

"You are quite adamant for being so aged. However, I am not walking fifty blocks to my home. I would rather face death by rusty fork."

"Okay, buddy, now listen to me. I'll make a bargain with you. You go out and push one of these wagons for an hour, and we'll call it quits."

"Don't I need clearance from the Health Department or something? I mean, I might have something beneath my fingernails that is very debilitating to the human system. Incidentally, do you get all of your vendors this way? Your hiring practices are hardly in step with contemporary policy. I feel as if I've been shanghaied. I am too apprehensive to ask how you go about firing your employees."

"Just don't ever try to rob a hot dog man again."

"You've just made your point. Actually, you have made two of them, literally in my throat and muffler. I hope that you are prepared to compensate for the muffler. There are no more of its kind. It was made in a small factory in England that was destroyed by the Luftwaffe. At the time it was rumored that the Luftwaffe was directed to strike directly at the factory in order to destroy British morale, for the Germans had seen Churchill wrapped in a muffler of this sort in a confiscated newsreel. For all I know, this may be the same one that Churchill was wearing in that particular Movietone. Today their value is somewhere in the thousands. It can also be worn as a shawl. Look."

"Well," the old man said finally, after watching Ignatius employ the muffler as a cummerbund, a sash, a cloak, and a pair of kilts, a sling for a broken arm, and a kerchief, "you ain't gonna do too much damage to Paradise Vendors in one hour."

"If the alternatives are jail or a pierced Adam's apple, I shall happily push one of your carts. Though I can't predict how far I'll go."

"Don't get me wrong, son. I ain't a bad guy, but you can only take so much. I spent ten years trying to make Paradise Vendors a reputable organization, but that ain't easy. People look down on hot dog vendors. They think I operate a business for bums. I got trouble finding decent vendors. Then when I find some nice guy, he goes out and gets himself mugged by hoodlums. How come God had to make it so tough for you?"

"We must not question His ways," Ignatius said.

"Maybe not, but I still don't get it."

"The writings of Boethius may give you some insight."

"I read Father Keller and Billy Graham in the paper every single day."

"Oh, my God!" Ignatius spluttered. "No wonder you are so lost."

"Here," the old man said, opening a metal locker near the stove. "Put this on."

He took what looked like a white smock out of the locker and handed it to Ignatius.

"What is this?" Ignatius asked happily. "It looks like an academic gown."

Ignatius slipped it over his head. On top of his overcoat, the smock made him look like a dinosaur egg about to hatch.

"Tie it at the waist with the belt."

"Of course not. These things are supposed to freely flow about the human form, although this one seems to provide little leeway. Are you sure that you don't have one in a larger size?

"Upon close scrutiny, I notice that this gown is rather yellow about the cuffs. I hope that these stains about the chest are ketchup rather than blood. The last wearer of this might have been stabbed by hoodlums."

"Here, put on this cap." The man gave Ignatius a little rectangle of white paper.

"I am certainly not wearing a paper cap. The one that I have is perfectly good and far more healthful."

"You can't wear a hunting cap. This is the Paradise vendor's uniform."

"I will not wear the paper cap! I am not going to die of pneumonia while playing this little game for you. Plunge the fork into my vital organs, if you wish. I will not wear that cap. Death before dishonor and disease."

"Okay, drop it," the old man sighed. "Come on and take this cart here."

"Do you think that I am going to be seen on the streets with that damaged abomination?" Ignatius asked furiously, smoothing the vendor's smock over his body. "Give me that shiny one with the white sidewall tires."

"Awright, awright," the old man said testily. He opened the lid on the little well in the cart and with a fork slowly began transferring hot dogs from the pot to the little well in the cart. "Now I give you a dozen hot dogs." He opened another lid in the top of the metal bun. "I'm putting a package of buns in here. Got that?" He closed that lid and pulled upon a little side door cut in the shining red tin dog. "In here they got a little can of liquid heat keeps the hot dogs warm."

"My God," Ignatius said with some respect. "These carts are like Chinese puzzles. I suspect that I will continually be pulling at the wrong opening."

The old man opened still another lid cut in the rear of the hot dog.

"What's in there? A machine gun?"

"The mustard and ketchup's in here."

"Well, I shall give this a brave try, although I may sell someone the can of liquid heat before I get too far."

The old man rolled the cart to the door of the garage and said, "Okay, buddy, go ahead."

"Thank you so much," Ignatius replied and wheeled the big tin hot dog out onto the sidewalk. "I will be back promptly in an hour."

"Get off the sidewalk with that thing."

"I hope that you don't think I am going out into the traffic."

"You can get yourself arrested for pushing one of them things on the sidewalk."

"Good," Ignatius said. "If the police follow me, they might prevent a robbery."

Ignatius pushed slowly away from the headquarters of Paradise Vendors through the heavy pedestrian traffic that moved to either side of the big hot dog like waves on a ship's prow. This was a better way of passing time than seeing personnel managers, several of whom, Ignatius thought, had treated him rather viciously in the last few days. Since the movie houses were now off limits due to lack of funds, he would have had to drift, bored and aimless, around the business district until it seemed safe to return home. The people on the street looked at Ignatius, but no one bought. After he had gone half a block, he began calling, "Hot dogs! Hot dogs from Paradise!"

"Get in the street, pal," the old man cried somewhere behind him.

Ignatius turned the corner and parked the wagon against a building. Opening the various lids, he prepared a hot dog for himself and ravenously ate it. His mother had been in a violent mood all week, refusing to buy him any Dr. Nut, pounding on his door when he was trying to write, threatening to sell the house and move into an old folks' home. She described to Ignatius the courage of Patrolman Mancuso, who, against heavy odds, was *fighting* to retain his job, who *wanted* to work, who was making the best of his torture and exile in the bathroom at the bus station. Patrolman Mancuso's situation reminded Ignatius of the situation of Boethius when he was imprisoned by the emperor before being killed. To pacify his mother and to improve conditions at home, he had given her *The Consolation of Philosophy*, an English translation of the work that Boethius had written while unjustly imprisoned and had told her to give it to Patrolman Mancuso so that he might peruse it while sealed in his booth. "The book teaches us to accept that which we cannot change. It describes the plight of a just  man in an unjust society. It is the very basis for medieval thought. No doubt it will aid your patrolman during his moments of crisis," Ignatius had said benevolently. "Yeah?" Mrs. Reilly had asked. "Aw, that's sweet, Ignatius. Poor Angelo'll be glad to get this." For about a day, at least, the present to Patrolman Mancuso had brought a temporary peace to life on Constantinople Street.

When he had finished the first hot dog, Ignatius prepared and consumed another, contemplating other kindnesses that might postpone his having to go to work again. Fifteen minutes later, noticing that the supply of hot dogs in the little well was visibly diminishing, he decided in favor of abstinence for the moment. He began to push slowly down the street, calling again, "Hot dogs!"

George, who was wandering up Carondelet with an armload of packages wrapped in plain brown paper, heard the cry and went up to the gargantuan vendor.

"Hey, stop. Gimme one of these."

Ignatius looked sternly at the young boy who had placed himself in the wagon's path. His valve protested against the pimples, the surly face that seemed to hang from the long well-lubricated hair, the cigarette behind the ear, the aquamarine jacket, the delicate boots, the tight trousers that bulged offensively in the crotch in violation of all rules of theology and geometry.

"I am sorry," Ignatius snorted. "I have only a few frankfurters left, and I must save them. Please get out of my way."

"Save them? Who for?"

"That is none of your business, you waif. Why aren't you in school? Kindly stop molesting me. Anyway, I have no change."

"I got a quarter," the thin white lips sneered.

"I cannot sell you a frank, sir. Is that clear?"

"Whatsa matter with you, friend?"

"What's the matter with *me?* What's the matter with *you?* Are you unnatural enough to want a hot dog this early in the afternoon? My conscience will not let me sell you one. Just look at your loathsome complexion. You are a growing boy whose system needs to be surfeited with vegetables and orange juice and whole wheat bread and spinach and such. I, for one, will not contribute to the debauchery of a minor."

"Whadda you talking about? Sell me one of them

hot dogs. I'm hungry. I ain't had no lunch."

"No!" Ignatius screamed so furiously that the passersby stared. "Now get away from me before I run over you with this cart."

George pulled open the lid of the bun compartment and said, "Hey, you got plenty stuff in here. Fix me a weenie."

"Help!" Ignatius screamed, suddenly remembering the old man's warnings about robberies. "Someone is stealing my buns! Police!"

Ignatius backed up the cart and rammed it into George's crotch.

"Ouch! Watch out there, you nut."

"Help! Thief!"

"Shut up, for Christ's sake," George said and slammed the door. "You oughta be locked up, you big fruit. You know that?"

"What?" Ignatius screamed. "What impertinence was that?"

"You big crazy fruit," George snarled more loudly

and slouched away, the taps on his heels scraping the sidewalk. "Who wants to eat anything your fruity hands touched?"

"How dare you scream obscenities at me. Someone grab that boy," Ignatius said wildly as George disappeared into the crowds of pedestrians farther down the street. "Someone with some decency grab that juvenile delinquent. That filthy little minor. Where is his respect? That little guttersnipe must be lashed until he collapses!"

A woman in the group around the mobile hot dog said, "Ain't that awful? Where they get them hot dog vendors from?"

"Bums. They all bums," someone answered her.

"Wine is what it is. They all crazy from wine if you ast me. They shouldn't let people like him out on the street."

"Is my paranoia getting completely out of hand," Ignatius asked the group, "or are you mongoloids really talking about me?"

"Let him alone," someone said. "Look at them eyes."

"What's wrong with my eyes?" Ignatius asked viciously.

"Let's get outta here."

"Please do." Ignatius replied, his lips quivering, and prepared another hot dog to quiet his trembling nervous system. With shaking hands, he held the foot of red plastic and dough to his mouth and slipped it in two inches at a time. The active chewing massaged his throbbing head. When he had shoved in the last millimeter of crumb, he felt much calmer.

Grabbing the handle again, he shoved off up Carondelet Street, waddling slowly behind the cart. True to his promise to make it around the block, he turned again at the next corner and stopped by the worn granite walls of Gallier Hall to consume two more of the Paradise hot dogs before continuing on the last leg of his journey. When Ignatius turned the final corner and saw again the PARADISE VENDORS, INC., sign hanging out over the sidewalk of Poydras

Street at an angle, he broke into a relatively brisk trot that brought him panting through the doors of the garage.

"Help!" Ignatius breathed pitifully, bumping the tin hot dog over the low cement sill of the garage.

"What happened, pal? I thought you was supposed to stay out a whole hour."

"We're both fortunate that I have returned at all. I am afraid that they have struck again."

"Who?"

"The syndicate. Whoever they are. Look at my hands." Ignatius shoved two paws into the man's face. "My entire nervous system is on the brink of revolt against me for subjecting it to such trauma. Ignore me if I suddenly go into a state of shock."

"What the hell happened?"

"A member of the vast teen-age underground besieged me on Carondelet Street."

"You was robbed?" the old man asked excitedly.

"Brutally. A large and rusty pistol was placed at

my temples. Actually, was pressed directly upon a pressure point, causing the blood to stop circulating on the left side of my head for quite a while."

"On Carondelet Street at this time of day? Nobody stopped it?"

"Of course no one stopped it. People encourage this sort of thing. They probably derive some sort of pleasure from the spectacle of a poor and struggling vendor's being publicly humiliated. They probably respected the boy's initiative."

"What did he look like?"

"A thousand other youths. Pimples, pompadour, adenoids, the standard adolescent equipment. There might have been something else like a birthmark or trick knee. I really can't recall. After the pistol had been thrust against my head, I fainted from lack of circulation in the brain and from

fright. While I was lying in a heap on the sidewalk, he apparently ransacked the wagon."

"How much money did he get?"

"Money? No money was stolen. After all, there was no money to steal, for I had not been able to vend even one of these delicacies. He stole the hot dogs.

"Yes. However, he apparently didn't take them all. When I had recovered, I checked the wagon. There are still one or two left, I think."

"I never heard of nothing like this."

"Perhaps he was very hungry. Perhaps some vitamin deficiency in his growing body was screaming for appeasement. The human desire for food and sex is relatively equal. If there are armed rapes, why should there not be armed hot dog thefts? I see nothing unusual in the matter."

"You're full of bullshit."

PETRONIUS

The Satyricon

UR APPLAUSE WAS interrupted by the second course, which did not by any means come up to our expectations. Still the oddity of the thing drew the eyes of all. An immense circular tray bore the twelve signs of the zodiac displayed round the circumference, on each of which the Manoiple or Arranger had placed a dish of suitable and appropriate viands; on the Ram ram's-head pease, on the Bull a piece of beef, on the Twins fried testicles and kidneys, on the Crab simply a Crown, on the Lion African figs, on a Virgin a sow's haslet, on Libra a balance with a tart in one scale and a cheese-cake in the other, on Scorpio a small sea-fish, on Sagittarius an eye-seeker, on Capricornus a lobster, on Aquarius a wild goose, on Pisces two mullets. In the middle was a sod of green turf cut to shape and support-ing a honeycomb. Meanwhile an Egyptian slave was carrying bread round in a miniature oven of silver, crooning to himself in a horrible voice a song in praise of wine and laserpitium.

Seeing us look rather blank at the idea of attack-ing such common fare, Trimalchio cried, "I pray you gentlemen, begin; the best of your dinner is before you." No sooner had he spoken than four fellows ran prancing in, keeping time to the music, and whipped off the top part of the tray. This done, we beheld underneath, on a second tray in fact, stuffed capons, a sow's paps, and as a centrepiece a hare fitted with wings to represent Pegasus. We noticed besides four figures of Marsyas, one at each corner of the tray, carrying little wine-skins which spouted out peppered fish-sauce over the fishes swimming in the Channel of the dish.

We all join in the applause started by the domestics and laughingly fall to on the choice viands. Trimalchio, as pleased as anybody with a device of the sort, now called out, "Cut!" Instantly the Carver advanced, and posturing in time to the music, sliced up the joint with such antics you might have thought him a jockey struggling to pull off a chariot-race to the thunder of the organ. Yet all the while Trimalchio kept repeating in a wheedling voice, "Cut! Cut!" For my part, suspecting there was some pretty jest connected with this everlasting reiteration of the word, I made no bones about asking the question of the guest who sat immediately above me. He had often witnessed similar scenes and told me at once, "You see the man who is carving; well; his name is Cut. The master is calling and commanding him at one and the same time."

Unable to eat any more, I now turned towards my neighbour in order to glean what information I could, and after indulging in a string of general remarks, presently asked him, "Who is that lady bustling up and down the room yonder?" "Trimalchio's lady," he replied; "her name is Fortunata, and she counts her coin by the bushelful! Before? what was she before? Why! my dear Sir! saving your respect, you would have been mighty sorry to take bread from her hand. Now, by hook or by crook, she's got to heaven, and is Trimalchio's factotum. In fact if she told him it was dark night at high noon, he'd believe her. The man's rolling in riches, and really can't tell what he has and what he hasn't got; still his good lady looks keenly after everything, and is on the spot where you least expect to see her. She's temperate, sober and well advised, but she has a sharp tongue of her own and chatters like a magpie between the bed-curtains. When she likes a man, she likes him; and when she doesn't, well! she doesn't.

"As for Trimalchio, his lands reach as far as the kites fly, and his money breeds money. I tell you, he has more coin lying idle in his porter's lodge than would make another man's whole fortune. Slaves! why, heaven and earth! I don't believe one in ten knows his own master by sight. For all that, there's never a one of the fine fellows a word of his wouldn't send scutting into the nearest rat-hole. And don't you imagine he ever buys anything; every mortal thing is home grown,—wool, rosin, pepper; call for hen's milk and he'd supply you! As a matter of fact his wool was not first rate originally; but he purchased rams at Tarentum and so improved the breed. To get homemade Attic honey he had bees imported direct from Athens, hoping at the same time to benefit the native insects a bit by a cross with the Greek fellows. Why! only the other day he wrote to India for mushroom spawn. He has not a single mule but was got by a wild ass. You see all these mattresses; never a one that is not stuffed with the finest wool, purple or scarlet as the case may be. Lucky, lucky dog!

"And look you, don't you turn up your nose at the other freedmen, his fellows. They're very warm men. You see the one lying last on the last couch yonder? He's worth his eight hundred thousand any of these days. A self-made man; once upon a time he carried wood on his own two shoulders. They do say,—I don't know how true it may be, but I've been told so—he snatched an Incubo's hat, and so discovered a treasure. I grudge no man's good fortune, whatever God has seen good to give him. He'll still take a box o' the ear for all that, and keeps a keen eye on the main chance. Only the other day he placarded his house with this bill:

C. POMPEIUS DIOGENES

IS PREPARED TO LET HIS GARRET

From July First,

Having Bought the House Himself.

"But the other man yonder, occupying a freed-man's place, what of him? Was he originally very well to do?" "I have not a word to say against him. He was master once of a cool million, but he came to sad grief. I don't suppose he has a hair on his head unmortgaged. Not that it was any fault of his; there never was a better man, but his rascally freedmen swindled him out of everything. Let me tell you, when the hospitable pot stops boiling, and fortune has once taken the turn, friends soon make themselves scarce." "What was the honourable calling he fol-lowed, that you see him brought to this?" "He was an undertaker. He used to dine like a King,—boars in pastry, cakes of every sort and game galore, cooks and pastry-cooks without end. More wine was spilt under his table than another man has in his cellar. A dream—not a life for a mere mortal man! Even when his affairs were getting shaky, for fear his creditors might think he was in difficulties, he posted this notice of sale:

C. JULIUS PROCULUS

WILL PUT UP TO AUCTION

AN ASSORTMENT

OF HIS SUPERFLUOUS FURNITURE."

This agreeable gossip was here interrupted by Trimalchio; for the second course had now been removed, and the company being merry with wine began to engage in general conversation. Our host then, lying back on his elbow and addressing the company, said, "I hope you will all do justice to this wine; you must make the fish swim again. Come, come, do you suppose I was going to rest content with the dinner you saw boxed up under the cover of the tray just now? 'Is Ulysses no better known?' Well, well! even at table we mustn't forget our scholarship. Peace to my worthy patron's bones, who was

pleased to make me a man amongst men. For truly
there is nothing can be set before me that will non-
plus me by its novelty. For instance the meaning of
that tray just now can be easily enough explained.
This heaven in which dwell the twelve gods resolves
itself into twelve different configurations, and
presently becomes the Ram. So whosoever is born
under this sign has many flocks and herds and much
wool, a hard head into the bargain, a shameless brow
and a sharp horn. Most of your schoolmen and petti-
foggers are born under this sign."

We recommended the learned expounder's grace-
ful erudition, and he went on to add: "Next the whole
sky becomes Bull; then are born obstinate fellows and
neatherds and such as think of nothing but filling
their own bellies. Under the Twins are born horses in
a pair, oxen in a yoke, men blessed with a sturdy
brace of testicles, all who manage to keep in with
both sides. I was born under the Crab myself.
Wherefore I stand on many feet, and have many pos-

sessions both by sea and land; for the Crab is equally adapted to either element. And this is why I never put anything on that sign, so as not to eclipse my horoscope. Under the Lion are born great eaters and wasters, and all who love to domineer; under the Virgin, women and runaways and jailbirds; under the Scales, butchers and perfumers and all retail traders; under the Scorpion, poisoners and cut-throats; under the Archer, squint-eyed folks, who look at the greens and whip off with the bacon; under Capricorn, the 'horny-handed sons of toil'; under Aquarius or the Waterman, innkeepers and pumpkin-heads; under Pisces, or the Fishes, fine cooks and fine talkers. Thus the world goes round like a mill, and is for ever at some mischief, whether making men or marring them. But about the sod of turf you see in the middle, and the honeycomb atop of it, I have a good reason to show too. Our mother Earth is in the middle, round-about like an egg, and has all good things in her inside, like a honeycomb!"

"Clever! clever!" we cry in chorus, and with hands uplifted to the ceiling, swear Hipparchus and Aratus were not to be named in the same breath with him. This lasted till fresh servants entered and spread carpets before the couches, embroidered with pictures of fowling nets, prickers with their hunting spears, and sporting gear of all kinds. We were still at a loss what to expect when a tremendous shout was raised outside the doors, and lo! and behold, a pack of Laconian dogs came careering round and round the very table.  These were succeeded by another huge tray, on which lay a wild boar of the largest size, with a cap on its head, while from the tushes hung two little baskets of woven palm leaves, one full of Syrian dates, the other of Theban. Round it were little piglets of baked sweetmeat, as if at suck, to show it was a sow we had before us; and these were gifts to be taken home with them by the guests.

To carve the dish however, it was not this time our friend Cut who appeared, the same who had dismembered the capons, but a great bearded fellow, wearing leggings and a shaggy jerkin. Drawing his hunting knife, he made a furious lunge and gashed open the boar's flank, from which there flew out a number of field-fares. Fowlers stood ready with their rods and immediately caught the birds as they fluttered about the table. Then Trimalchio directed each guest to be given his bird, and this done, added "Look what elegant acorns this wild-wood pig fed on." Instantly slaves ran to the baskets that were suspended from the animal's tushes and divided the two kind of dates in equal proportions among the diners.

Meantime, sitting as I did a little apart, I was led into a thousand conjectures to account for the boar's being brought in with a cap on. So after exhausting all sorts of absurd guesses, I resolved to ask my former "philosopher and friend" to explain the difficulty that tormented me so. "Why!" said he, "your own servant could tell you that much. Riddle? it's as plain as day-light. The boar was presented with his freedom at yes-terday's dinner; he appeared at the end of the meal and the company gave him his congé. Therefore today he comes back to table as a freedman." I cursed my own stupidity, and asked no more questions, for fear of their thinking I had never dined with good company before.

We were all conversing, when a pretty boy entered, his head wreathed with vine-leaves and ivy, announcing himself now as Bromius, anon as Lyaeus and Evous. He proceeded to hand round grapes in a small basket, and recited in the shrillest of voices some verses of his mas-ter's composition. Trimalchio turned round at the sound, and, "Dionysus," said he, "be free [Liber]!" The lad snatched the cap from the boar's head and stuck it on his own. Then Trimalchio went on again, "Well! you'll not deny," he cried, "I have a Father Liber [a freeborn father] of my own." We praised Trimalchio's joke, and heartily kissed the fortunate lad, as he went round the company to receive our congratulations.

DIANE MASON

Feast

HE FEAST WAS called for 2 A.M., when everyone was so tired that it was sleep, not food, they craved the most. The waiters, wearing tuxedos of limpid green and cummerbunds of pumpkin, marched in formation, carrying the foods the hostess had chosen, all aligned on silver trays in shapes of figure eights and triangles, instead of the standard ovals.

The first platters bore the soups and rolls: sweet twists of dough browned lightly at the curves; poppyseed breadsticks and sesame-seed kaisers; crisp toasts and pumpernickels and pita breads like skullcaps. The soups were green pea, the same color as the waiters' jackets, and another pot held a pink chowder, lumpy with clams and sprinkled with paprika. Behind that cauldron sat another, filled with overspiced minestrone, crammed so full of meat and vegetables that it was hardly fluid. Finally, a cold potato soup, a vichyssoise, white and translucent, settling beside its steaming cousins.

The next platters were fruits and salads, but these salads were of meats and starches and seafoods, sodden with dressing, clinging to the sides of the huge wooden bowls. One bowl of greens had been peppered with chickpeas and cherry tomatoes, and soaked with olive oil and Tabasco. The spoons dripped. The fruit was overlarge and swollen; the oranges had unborn twins of themselves grafted onto their navels, and the twins were segmented and seedless, too. The apples were lumped at the bottom, and were so sweet they stung the teeth. The bananas were the size and shape of cucumbers, and a waxy, uniform yellow.

The main course was half a cow, split from nose to anus and served in that form, except that the chef had been obliged to saw it laterally in half in order to fit it in his ovens. He charged extra for this. The chef then reassembled the cow, using suture floss to rejoin the two segments, and warned his servers not to cut too closely to the stitches. Some of the meat was crisped and black, while close to the bone it was gooey crimson, the tendons shining through. Where it was well cooked, the flesh fell effortlessly from the bone.

The sounds of eating filled the hall as the guests accepted plates of soup and baskets of bread, and the waiters served wines from Italy, Spain, and Chile, in glassware from France, cut in a simple style but with a stem that bit into the fingers. Conversation was minimal. Everyone chewed noisily, with mouths open; they slurped and sighed and picked crumbs from their laps. Their teeth smacked against their gums as they cleared debris from the recesses of their mouths. The beef began to dwindle as people requested seconds. The cow's bones emerged, shreds of mud-colored meat clinging to the ribs.

The server took an ax and severed the cow's half-head from its half-neck, neatly at the second vertebra, and set it on a platter for the waiters to take away. The waiters were serving dollops of vegetables to complement the beef: okra, pickled beets of a grape-jelly purple, and a mixture of green peas and kernel corn in a thin, buttery sauce. The edge having been taken off their hunger, the people began to converse, their panic to eat now abated. They took smaller bites, laughing with their mouths full, revealing the chewed, fluffy, pan-roasted potatoes.

When the sorbet arrived, many mistook it for dessert, and thought the dinner was ending. But after the sorbet, which was pineapple and white grape, came eggs Florentine, with its spinach melting into the viscous flesh of the poached eggs. The guests picked bits of grapeskin the consistency of corneas from their teeth, using the toothpicks provided, and with the ice barely settled in their stomachs, commenced on the eggs. Soon their gastrointestinal tracts contracted, and people excused themselves, heading to the lavatories and powder rooms with bowels rumbling conversationally. The flushing of toilets was heard above the sound of the espresso machine.

As the waiters brought coffee, the master of ceremonies rose and greeted the guests, and thanked the hostess, who rose from her chair and bowed from the

waist. The master then informed the guests that the sweet-and-sour was about to appear, and would they content themselves in camaraderie until the chef had things in order.

The kitchen was in pandemonium. Metal clashed: lids on lids; serving spoons were dropped into pots and on the tile floor, clattering against the baseboards. The deep fryers boiled over, spilling oil onto the burners, and flames burst into the air, singeing the sous-chefs' hands. The potboys cowered. The chef was florid. The sweet-and-sour caught fire, which, although dramatic, was not part of the plan; the chef seized the bottle of triple-x brandy and doused the flames with a splash of its contents. The sweet-and-sour exploded into a neon ball. The chef handed the residue to the potboys and told them to serve it up.

The guests were full, but the food continued. A green salad arrived, with crescent moons of celery and shards of sweet pepper, and outer leaves of iceberg and romaine lettuce wilting from the warmth. Each salad was presented in a crystal bowl, and the glasses were never left empty. It seemed to the guests that they had been eating for a very long time, but none had the ill manners to check their watches. A blood pudding, filled with whitish lumps that fell open at the touch of the knife, followed.

The speeches began; the guests were again welcomed; each speaker had something eloquent and relevant to say. The waiters brought the aperitifs in tiny, blue-bottomed glasses, and the speeches concluded, the head table leading the applause. The windows were opened by waiters bearing long metal poles, and the stiff, stale air circulated. Cigarettes were lit, and quickly extinguished. More food was being brought.

It was custard of tapioca, dyed baby blue and garnished with carrot curls. But by then the hardiest of gluttons were slowing, the spoons dipped with less and less gusto. Plates of morels drizzled with butter were distributed by the now-jacketless waiters, whose white dress shirts had stains of gray sweat spreading as far as their waists. People began to talk of leaving; women organized their purses. As each tray was carried from the kitchen, a belch of steam and smoke poured from the squalor, and the chef could be heard screaming.

And still the food came. It came in buckets, in pots, and impaled on swords; it seeped from the ceiling and oozed from underfoot. It burst into the room in the arms of sweating servers, whose ties hung brokenly from their throats, and whose cummerbunds were stained with grease. The guests shifted anxiously. Surely there couldn't be much more; surely the end must be coming soon. But the courses were now oddly timed; there had been aperitifs in mid-meal, and that sherbet thing, with the sticky bits of grapeskin, hadn't that been a dessert? Or was it the tapioca? They looked at their plates and their glasses, filled again. The waiters closed the windows.

People began to knock things over in their nervousness, spilling salt and glasses of burgundy. Food and dishes hit the floor, causing the waiters to skid and overturn their trays. Entire platters spilled onto the guests; women's hairdos were ruined.

By the time the pastries arrived on wheeled carts, the waiters were naked. They used ivory tongs to offer cakes of a thousand layers to the patrons, not waiting for a reply before placing two, three, or four selections at each place. Some guests wept and pushed the cakes onto the floor. The waiters replaced the pastries, piling meringue with berries and chocolate and cream and sauce and spice and crumbs and sugar and honey and syrup and molasses and mincemeat and mocha and preserves and cashews and mangoes and figs, and then left, saying, "Enjoy your meal."

The guests looked at each other and recalled the days of their lives when they had walked the city streets eating ice cream in simple rolled cones; days when they had worn aprons saying "Kiss the Cook" as they fried segments of slaughtered pig over an open fire, sending smudges of greasy fumes into the firmament. They had entered buildings filled hip-deep with fruit and grains and vegetables and legumes and fungi, and they had bought these things and taken them home, never noticing what a famine plenty can disguise.

HENRY FAIRLIE

Gluttony or Gula

ATCH A GLUTTONOUS man at his food. His napkin is tucked in his collar and spread across his paunch, announcing the seriousness of the business in which he is engaged. His bulging face and popping eyes are fixed on his plate. Only occasionally does he look up at his companions with a glazed look. His mouth has only one function, as an orifice into which to push his food. Now and then he may grunt at what someone has said. Otherwise he stuffs. He is like a hog at its swill. He may ignore his companions; but they cannot ignore him. Even if they can avert their eyes from the spectacle—the swamp in his mouth, where the tide ebbs and flows, the seepage from its corners—they are unable to block their ears to the noise. He sucks each spoonful through his teeth as if it were the Sargasso Sea. He does not chew his meat but champs and chomps, crunches and craunches. He crams, gorges, wolfs, and bolts. He might as well be alone. As with all the sins, Gluttony makes us solitary. We place ourselves apart, even at a table of sharing.

Ben Jonson

Hymn to the Belly

OOM! ROOM! MAKE room for the
bouncing Belly,
First father of sauce and deviser of jelly;
Prime master of arts and the giver of wit,
That found out the excellent engine, the spit,
The plow and the flail, the mill and the hopper,
The hutch and the boulter, the furnace and copper,
The oven, the bavin, the mawkin, the peel,
The hearth and the range, the dog and the wheel.
He, he first invented the hogshead and tun,

The gimlet and vise too, and taught 'em to run;

And since, with the funnel and hippocras bag,

He's made of himself that now he cries swag;

Which shows, though the pleasure be but of four inches,

Yet he is a weasel, the gullet that pinches

Of any delight, and not spares from his back

Whatever to make of the belly a sack.

Hail, hail, plump paunch! O the founder of taste,

For fresh meats or powdered, or pickle or paste!

Devourer of broiled, baked, roasted or sod!

And emptier of cups, be they even or odd!

All which have now made thee so wide i' the waist,

As scarce with no pudding thou art to be laced;

But eating and drinking until thou dost nod,

Thou break'st all thy girdles and break'st forth a god.

WOODY ALLEN

Notes from the Overfed

AM FAT. I am disgustingly fat. I am the fattest human I know. I have nothing but excess poundage all over my body. My fingers are fat. My wrists are fat. My eyes are fat. (Can you imagine fat eyes?) I am hundreds of pounds overweight. Flesh drips from me like hot fudge off a sundae. My girth has been an object of disbelief to everyone who's seen me. There is no question about it, I'm a regular fatty. Now, the reader may ask, are there advantages or disadvantages to being built like a planet? I do not mean to be facetious or speak in paradoxes, but I must answer that fat in itself is above bourgeois morality. It is simply fat. That fat could have a value of its own, that fat could be, say, evil or pitying, is, of course, a joke. Absurd! For what is fat after all but an accumulation of pounds? And what are pounds? Simply an aggregate composite of cells. Can a cell be moral? Is a cell beyond good or evil? Who knows— they're so small. No, my friend, we must never attempt to distinguish between good fat and bad fat. We must train ourselves to confront the obese without judging, without thinking this man's fat is first-rate fat and this poor wretch's is grubby fat.

Take the case of K. This fellow was porcine to such a degree that he could not fit through the average door-frame without the aid of a crowbar. Indeed, K. would not think to pass from room to room in a conventional dwelling without first stripping completely and then buttering himself. I am no stranger to the insults K. must have borne from passing gangs of young rowdies. How frequently he must have been stung by cries of "Tubby!" and "Blimp!" How it must have hurt when the governor of the province turned to him on the Eve of Michaelmas and said, before many dignitaries, "You hulking pot of *kasha!*"

Then one day, when K. could stand it no longer, he dieted. Yes, dieted! First sweets went. Then bread, alcohol, starches, sauces. In short, K. gave up the very stuff that makes a man unable to tie his shoelaces without help from the Santini Brothers. Gradually he began to slim down. Rolls of flesh fell from his arms and legs. Where once he looked roly-poly, he suddenly appeared in public with a normal build. Yes, even an attractive build. He seemed the happiest of men. I say "seemed," for eighteen years later, when he was near death and fever raged throughout his slender frame, he was heard to cry out, "My fat! Bring me my fat! Oh, please! I must have my fat! Oh, somebody lay some avoirdupois on me! What a fool I've been. To part with one's fat! I

must have been in league with the Devil!" I think that
the point of the story is obvious.

Now the reader is probably thinking, Why, then, if
you are Lard City, have you not joined a circus?
Because—and I confess this with no small embarrassment—I cannot leave the house. I cannot go out
because I cannot get my pants on. My legs are too
thick to dress. They are the living result of more
corned beef than there is on Second Avenue—I would
say about twelve thousand sandwiches per leg. And not
all lean, even though I specified. One thing is certain:
If my fat could speak, it would probably speak of man's
intense loneliness—with, oh, perhaps a few additional
pointers on how to make a sailboat out of paper. Every
pound on my body wants to be heard from, as do

Chins Four through Twelve inclusive. My fat is strange fat. It has seen much. My calves alone have lived a lifetime. Mine is not happy fat, but it is real fat. It is not fake fat. Fake fat is the worst fat you can have, although I don't know if the stores still carry it.

But let me tell you how it was that I became fat. For I was not always fat. It is the Church that has made me thus. At one time I was thin—quite thin. So thin, in fact, that to call me fat would have been an error in perception. I remained thin until one day—I think it was my twentieth birthday—when I was having tea and cracknels with my uncle at a fine restaurant. Suddenly my uncle put a question to me. "Do you believe in God?" he asked. "And if so, what do you think He weighs?" So saying, he took a long and luxurious draw on his cigar and, in that confident, assured manner he has cultivated, lapsed into a coughing fit so violent I thought he would hemorrhage.

"I do not believe in God," I told him. "For if there is a God, then tell me, Uncle, why is there poverty and baldness? Why do some men go through life immune to a thousand mortal enemies of the race, while others get a migraine that lasts for weeks? Why are our days numbered and not, say, lettered? Answer me, Uncle. Or have I shocked you?"

I knew I was safe in saying this, because nothing ever shocked the man. Indeed, he had seen his chess tutor's mother raped by Turks and would have found the whole incident amusing had it not taken so much time.

"Good nephew," he said, "there is a God, despite what you think, and He is everywhere. Yes! Everywhere!"

"Everywhere, Uncle? How can you say that when you don't even know for sure if we exist? True, I am touching your wart at this moment, but could that not be an illusion? Could not all life be an illusion? Indeed, are there not certain sects of holy men in the East who are convinced that *nothing* exists outside their minds except for the Oyster Bar at Grand

Central Station? Could it not be simply that we are alone and aimless, doomed to wander in an indifferent universe, with no hope of salvation, nor any prospect except misery, death, and the empty reality of eternal nothing?"

I could see that I made a deep impression on my uncle with this, for he said to me, "You wonder why you're not invited to more parties! Jesus, you're morbid!" He accused me of being nihilistic and then said, in that cryptic way the senile have, "God is not always where one seeks Him, but I assure you, dear nephew, He is everywhere. In these cracknels, for instance." With that, he departed, leaving me his blessing and a check that read like the tab for an aircraft carrier.

I returned home wondering what it was he meant by that one simple statement "He is everywhere. In these cracknels, for instance." Drowsy by then, and out of sorts, I lay down on my bed and took a brief nap. In that time, I had a dream that was to change my life forever. In the dream, I am strolling in the country, when I suddenly notice I am hungry. Starved, if you will. I come upon a restaurant and I enter. I order the open-hot-roast-beef sandwich and a side of French. The waitress, who resembles my landlady (a thoroughly insipid woman who reminds one instantly of some of the hairier lichens), tries to tempt me into ordering the chicken salad, which doesn't look fresh. As I am conversing with this woman, she turns into a twenty-four-piece starter set of silverware. I become hysterical with laughter, which suddenly turns to tears and then into a serious ear infection. The room is suffused with a radiant glow, and I see a shimmering figure approach on a white steed. It is my podiatrist, and I fall to the ground with guilt.

Such was my dream. I awoke with a tremendous sense of well-being. Suddenly I was optimistic. Everything was clear. My uncle's statement reverberated to the core of my very existence. I went to the kitchen and started to eat. I ate everything in sight.

Cakes, breads, cereals, meat, fruits. Succulent choco-
lates, vegetables in sauce, wines, fish, creams and noo-
dles, éclairs, and wursts totalling in excess of sixty
thousand dollars. If God is everywhere, I had concluded, then He is in food. Therefore, the more I ate
the godlier I would become. Impelled by this new
religious fervor, I glutted myself like a fanatic. In six
months, I was the holiest of holies, with a heart
entirely devoted to my prayers and a stomach that
crossed the state line by itself. I last saw my feet one
Thursday morning in Vitebsk, although for all I know
they are still down there. I ate and
ate and grew and grew. To reduce
would have been the greatest folly.
Even a sin! For when we lose
twenty pounds, dear reader (and I
am assuming you are not as large
as I), we may be losing the twenty
best pounds we have! We may be
losing the pounds that contain our

genius, our humanity, our love and honesty or, in the case of one inspector general I knew, just some unsightly flab around the hips.

Now, I know what you are saying. You are saying this is in direct contradiction to everything—yes, everything—I put forth before. Suddenly I am attributing to neuter flesh, values! Yes, and what of it? Because isn't life that very same kind of contradiction? One's opinion of fat can change in the same manner that the seasons change, that our hair changes, that life itself changes. For life is change and fat is life, and fat is also death. Don't you see? Fat is everything! Unless, of course, you're overweight.

WILLIAM SHAKESPEARE

King Henry the Fourth

Falstaff:

 WOULD YOU HAD BUT THE WIT: 'TWERE
better than your dukedom. Good faith, this
same young sober-blooded boy doth not love
me; nor a man cannot make him laugh; but
that's no marvel, he drinks no wine. There's never none of
these demure boys come to any proof; for thin drink doth so
over-cool their blood, and making many fish-meals, that
they fall into a kind of male green-sickness; and then, when
they marry, they get wenches. They are generally fools and
cowards, which some of us should be too but for inflamma-

tion. A good sherris-sack hath a two-fold operation in it. It ascends me into the brain; dries me there all the foolish and dull and crudy vapours which environ it; makes it apprehensive, quick, forgetive, full of nimble, fiery and delectable shapes; which, deliver'd o'er to the voice, the tongue, which is the birth, becomes excellent wit. The second property of your excellent sherris is, the warming of the blood; which, before cold and settled, left the liver white and pale, which is the badge of pusillanimity and cowardice: but the sherris warms it and makes it course from the inwards to the parts extreme. It illumineth the face, which, as a beacon, gives warning to all the rest of this little kingdom, man, to arm; and then the vital commoners and inland petty spirits muster me all to their captain, the heart, who, great and puffed up with this retinue, doth any deed of courage; and this valour comes of sherris. So that skill in the weapon is nothing without sack, for that sets it a-work; and learning, a mere hoard of gold kept by a devil till sack commences it and sets it in act and use. Hereof comes it that Prince Harry is valiant; for the cold blood he did naturally inherit of his father, he hath, like lean, sterile, and bare land, manured, husbanded, and tilled, with excellent endeavour of drinking good and good store of fertile sherris, that he is become very hot and valiant. If I had a thousand sons, the first human principle I would teach them should be, to forswear thin potations and to addict themselves to sack.

JOHN POWERS

Sinfully Good

'VE ALWAYS THOUGHT gluttony has gotten a bad rap. I'm not even sure it should be one of the Deadly Sins. Gluttons tend to be smiling, passive sorts. They give employment to thousands of butchers, bakers and cardiologists, and they invariably clean their plates. The angry, the envious and the proud could all learn something from the gluttonous. I don't consider myself a glutton, but I've been fantasizing about becoming one ever since I read *A*

Christmas Carol as a boy. The Ghost of Christmas Present, perched with holly crown and torch atop his splendid cornucopia, is my gustatory idol:

> Heaped up on the floor, to form a kind of throne, were turkeys, geese, game, poultry, brawn, great joints of meat, sucking-pigs, long wreaths of sausages, mince-pies, plum-puddings, barrels of oysters, red-hot chestnuts, cherry-cheeked apples, juicy oranges, luscious pears, immense twelfth-cakes and seething bowls of punch that made the chamber dim with their delicious steam.

Once a year, I will watch *Tom Jones*, fast-forwarding to the eating scene with Mrs. Waters at the inn—the game birds rent asunder with bare hands, oysters sucked straight from the shells, pear juice dribbling down chins. I have a tape of "Babette's Feast" and I can recite Babe Ruth's favorite midnight snack from memory: half a dozen club sandwiches, a platter of pig's knuckles, a pitcher of beer and a fat black cigar.

I don't know if I could match Ruth's prodigious appetite, but I wouldn't mind trying—at least once, anyway. But it would have to be on Father's Day, when indulgences are granted in the name of paternal homage. And I would have to spread the eating and drinking throughout the day (and evening), interspersed with strolling, dozing, contemplation and inspirational reading. It isn't gluttony if you pace yourself. Brillat-Savarin said that. Or maybe it was Diamond Jim Brady.

The 20,000-calorie Father's Day begins at 8 o'clock as I wake to the breeze and birdsong wafting through the open window. Before rising, I reach over

to the nightstand for a literary appetizer from *At Swim-Two-Birds*, by Flann O'Brien:

They also did not hesitate to promise him sides of hairy bacon, the mainstay and staff of life of the country classes, and lamb-chops still succulent with young blood, autumn-heavy yams from venerable stooping trees, bracelets and garlands of browned sausages and two baskets of peerless eggs fresh-collected, a waiting hand under the hen's bottom.

BREAKFAST: I've abandoned the idea of breakfast in bed because the balance of cups, dishes, cutlery and Sunday paper is too precarious and because I need to burn calories wherever possible. So I descend the stairs at a pace somewhere between a saunter and a canter. And so to table, and a jigger of Glenmorangie single-malt Scotch to clear the cobwebs and sweeten the pipes.

Then a dozen juice-swollen oranges squeezed into a frosted glass. For the centerpiece, a thick square of spicy Philadelphia scrapple fried to a light crunch, cushioned by a brace of farm-fresh double-yolked eggs turned with a gentle hand and adorned with a steaming buttermilk biscuit, fork-split and generously drizzled with creamery butter. To follow, an American-style *pain au chocolat*—that is, more *chocolat* than *pain*. It should be heated until the chocolate dribbles from either end in runny rivulets. Then a double handful of plump raspberries, burbling in heavy cream.

For coffee, an oversized mug of Viennese cinnamon, crowned with a dollop of whipped cream and a dash of nutmeg and accompanied by a chewy shortbread cookie in the shape of Father Time. To cleanse the palate, a wedge of chilled watermelon as thick as *War and Peace.*

At 10 o'clock, a brisk walk to and from the local horse-and-tomato farm with Debussy's "La Mer" on the headphones. Then a warm, soapy shower and a change of clothing—something looser and larger, with a generous waistband. As the noon hour approaches, a nibble from *The Dangerous Summer* by

Ernest Hemingway: "We drank sangria, red wine with fresh orange and lemon juice in it, served in big pitchers and ate local sausages to start with, fresh tuna, fresh prawns, and crisp fried octopus tentacles that tasted like lobster. Then some ate steaks and others roasted or grilled chicken with saffron yellow rice with pimentos and clams in it. It was a very moderate meal by Valencian standards and the woman who owned the place was worried that we would go away hungry."

LUNCHEON: A Campari and soda in a tall glass, sipped languidly out of doors while watching cardinals and doves swoop down on the feeder swinging from the cherry tree. To begin, a bowl of gazpacho, bobbing with garlic-drenched croutons and dusted with freshly ground pepper. Next up, a platter of grilled red peppers, onions, eggplant and tomatoes splashed with olive oil and garnished with anchovies. For the main, a fragrant paella, chockablock with clams, mussels, chorizo and chicken, washed down with a bottle of Rioja. Dessert is a prodigious and shimmering flan, surrounded with a squiggle of whipped cream and graced with a heavy spoonful of dulce de leche, the caramelly sacrament of Argentina. For a digestif, a glass of port and a Havana.

By now, the sun has crested over the birdbath and the body craves surcease—a hot-oil massage to the recorded sounds of a spring cloudburst in an Amazon rain forest. And then to sleep, perchance to dream. Upon awakening, two hours later, a sliver of *Toujours Provence*, by Peter Mayle:

And lunch continued as it had begun, *bien*. A flan of *foie gras* in a thick but delicate sauce of wild mushrooms and asparagus was followed by home-made sausages of Sisteron lamb and sage with a confiture of sweet red onions and, in a separate flat dish, a gratin of potato that was no thicker than my napkin, a single crisp layer that dissolved on the tongue.

DINNER: There is still enough strength left in the sun to summon forth visions of a shaded wicker chair in Aix, plane trees riffled by a late-day breeze, waiters bearing trays of pastis, ice and water. To prompt the appetite, two fingers' worth of Ricard, the licorice-flavored mother's milk of Marseille, dosed with two cubes and diluted with Evian. Then toasted chunks torn from a baguette and spread with  "Provençal peanut butter," i.e., the paste of Niçoise olives, capers, anchovies and garlic called tapenade.

The butterflied leg of lamb has been marinating overnight in its bath of olive oil, garlic, rosemary and mint. Now, it is laid gently over a bed of coals 30 minutes old, grilled to juicy pinkness in a dozen minutes and served alongside a small mountain of couscous and a bunch of asparagus, cooked for precisely 10 minutes, then spritzed with cold water. For wine, a bottle of velvety merlot. Dessert is crème brûlée, its crust delicate as the winter's first pane of ice, splintering under a light tap of the spoon. Courvoisier follows a double espresso.

With the stomach now pushing its bounds ever so slightly, an hour-long promenade is in order, just as the sky is changing color. M.F.K. Fisher strides alongside me, though she does not know it. Upon return, a torpid sprawl on the couch, with Mozart on the CD player. When I come to, the house is dark and, as Hemingway wrote, I am hungry in a simple way.

MIDNIGHT SNACK: Something very light. A smoked turkey leg, an icy bottle of Ballantine ale, a banana Popsicle and 12 inches of cinnamon-flavored dental floss. And so to bed.

FRAN LEBOWITZ

The Fran Lebowitz High Stress Diet and Exercise Program

 ACH YEAR MILLIONS of people attempt to shed excess pounds by dint of strenuous diet and exercise. They nibble carrot sticks, avoid starches, give up drinking, run around reservoirs, lift weights, swing from trapezes and otherwise behave in a manner that suggests an unhappy penchant for undue fanfare. All of this is, of course, completely unnecessary, for it is entirely possible—indeed, easy—to lose weight and tone up without the slightest effort of will. One has merely to conduct one's life in such a way that pounds and inches will disappear as of their own volition.

Magic, you say? Fantasy? Pie in the sky? Longing of the basest sort? Not at all, I assure you, not at all. No magic, no fantasy, no dreamy hopes of any kind. But a secret, ah yes, there is a secret. The secret of exploiting an element present in everyone's daily life, and using to its fullest advantage the almost inexhaustible resources available within.

That element? Stress. Yes, stress; plain, ordinary, everyday stress. The same type of stress that everyone has handy at any time of the day or night. Call it what you will: annoyance, work, pressure, art, love, it is stress nevertheless, and it is stress that will be your secret weapon as you embark on my foolproof program of physical fitness and bodily beauty.

Diet

The downfall of most diets is that they restrict your intake of food. This is, of course, galling, and inevitably leads to failure. The Fran Lebowitz High Stress Diet (T.F.L.H.S.D. for short) allows unlimited quantities of all foods. Naturally, space limitations make it impossible to furnish a complete list. If you can eat something that is not on this list—good luck to you.

Allowed Foods

Meat	Candy	Rice
Fish	Nuts	Spaghetti
Fowl	Cereal	Sugar
Eggs	Cookies	Syrup
Cheese	Crackers	Pizza
Butter	Honey	Potato Chips
Cream	Ice Cream	Pretzels
Mayonnaise	Ketchup	Pie
Fruits	Jam	Wine
Vegetables	Macaroni	Liquor
Bread	Milk	Beer
Cake	Pancakes	Ale

As you can see, T.F.L.H.S.D. permits you a variety of foods unheard of on most diets. And, as I have stated previously, quantity is of no concern. I ask only that you coordinate your eating with specific physical activities. This program is detailed below.

Equipment

You can proceed with The Fran Lebowitz High Stress Exercise Program (T.F.L.H.S.E.P.) without the purchase of special equipment; it calls for only those accouterments that you undoubtedly possess already. A partial list follows:

Cigarettes

Matches or lighter

A career

One or more lawyers

One agent or manager

At least one, but preferably two, extremely
    complicated love affairs

A mailing address

Friends

Relatives

A landlord

Necessary equipment will, of course, vary from person to person, but T.F.L.H.S.E.P. is flexible and can adapt to almost any situation. This is clearly seen in the sample one-day menu and exercise program that follows. It must be remembered that it is absolutely mandatory that you follow exercise instructions while eating.

Sample Menu and Program

BREAKFAST

Larger Orange Juice

6 Pancakes with Butter, Syrup and/or Jam

4 slices Bacon and/or 4 Sausage Links

Coffee with Cream and Sugar

11 Cigarettes

a. Take first bite of pancake.

b. Call agent. Discover that in order to write screen-play you must move to Los Angeles for three months and enter into a collaboration with a local writer who has to his credit sixteen episodes of *The Partridge Family*, one unauthorized biography of Ed McMahon, and the novelization of the projected sequel to *Missouri Breaks*. (Excellent for firming jawline.)

MIDMORNING SNACK

2 Glazed Doughnuts

Coffee with Cream and Sugar

8 Cigarettes

a. Take first sip of coffee.

b. Open mail and find final disconnect notice from telephone company, threatening letter from spouse of new flame and a note from a friend informing you that you have been recently plagiarized on network television. (Tones up fist area.)

LUNCH

2 Vodka and Tonics

Chicken Kiev

Pumpernickel Bread and Butter

Green Salad

White Wine

A Selection or Selections from the Pastry Tray

Coffee with Cream and Sugar

15 Cigarettes

a. Arrange to lunch with lawyer.

b. Take first bite of Chicken Kiev.

c. Inquire of lawyer as to your exact chances in litigation against CBS. (Flattens tummy fast.)

DINNER

3 Vodka and Tonics

Spaghetti al Pesto

Veal Piccata

Zucchini

Arugula Salad

Cheese Cake

Coffee with Cream and Sugar

Brandy

22 Cigarettes

a. Arrange to dine with a small group that includes three people with whom you are having clandestine love affairs, your younger sister from out of town, a business rival to whom you owe a great deal of money and two of the lawyers from CBS. It is always more fruitful to exercise with others. (Tightens up the muscles.)

As I have said, this is just a sample, and any combination of foods and exercises will work equally well. Your daily weight loss should average from between three to five pounds, depending largely on whether you are smoking a sufficient number of cigarettes. This is a common pitfall and close attention should be paid, for inadequate smoking is certain to result in a lessening of stress. For those of you who simply cannot meet your quota, it is imperative that you substitute other exercises, such as moving in downstairs from an aspiring salsa band and/or being terribly frank with your mother. If these methods fail, try eating while reading the *New York Times* Real Estate section. Admittedly, this is a drastic step and should not be taken before you have first warmed up with at least six pages of Arts and Leisure and one sexual encounter with a person vital to your career.

Occasionally I run across a dieter with an unusually stubborn weight problem. If you fall into this category, I recommend as a final desperate measure that you take your meals with a magazine editor who really and truly understands your work and a hairdresser who wants to try something new and interesting.

BILL BUFORD

Among the Thugs

N THE SPRING of 1984, Manchester United reached the semi-finals of the Cup-Winners Cup and was scheduled to play Turin's Juventus. The teams were to play twice: the first leg in Manchester, the second, two weeks later, in Turin. I had been intrigued by Manchester United for some time. Before May 1985, English teams had not been banned from playing on the continent; the supporters of Manchester United, however, had been: by the

team itself. I wanted to find out what these supporters were like. It seemed an extraordinary thing for
the team's management to ban its own fans.

The first match was on a Wednesday evening, and
I got a train to Manchester from London at around
three in the afternoon. Inside, it was the familiar sight:
people packed into the seats, on the floor, suspended
from the luggage racks, playing cards, rolling dice,
drinking unimaginable quantities of alcohol, steadily
sinking consciousness into a blurry stupor.

I walked from carriage to carriage, looking for one
of "them," and came across someone who was truly spec-
tacular to look at, qualifying for that special category of
human being—one of its most repellent specimens. He
had a fat, flat bulldog face and was extremely large. His
T-shirt had inched its way up his belly and was discol-
ored by something sticky and dark. The belly itself was
a tub of sorts, swirling, I would discover, with liters and
liters of lager, partly chewed chunks of fried potato, and
moist, undigested balls of overprocessed carbohydrate.

His arms—puffy, doughy things—were stained with tattoos. On his right biceps was an image of the Red Devils, the logo of the Manchester Union team; on his forearm, the Union Jack.

When I came upon him, he had just tossed an empty beer can into the overhead luggage rack—quite a few were there already—and had started in on a bottle of Tesco's vodka.

I introduced myself. I was writing about football supporters. Did he mind if I asked him some questions?

He stared at me. Then he said, "All Americans are wankers." And paused. "All journalists," he added, showing, perhaps, that his mind did not work along strictly nationalist lines, "are cunts."

We had established a rapport.

His name was Mick and, on arriving in Manchester, he rushed me across the street to a nearby pub for three pints of beer, drunk with considerable speed. I accompanied Mick to the match, where he led me to the Stretford End, the standing-room section of Old Trafford, packed, enclosed, so that the chants, showing an impressive command of history and linguistic dexterity—"Where were you in World War Two?"; *"Va fanculo"* ("Fuck off" in Italian)—were so amplified that it was hours before my ears stopped ringing: as I fell asleep that night I found myself relentlessly repeating the not especially somniferous slogan that "Mussolini was a wanker." At half time, Mick rushed off again for refreshment, which this time included two meat pies, a cheeseburger, and a plastic cup of something which Mick insisted was lager but whose temperature and consistency reminded me of vegetable soup. I couldn't touch it, and not losing a minute,

Mick—waste not, want not—drank mine as well. At the end of the match, Mick grabbed me by my sleeve, tugged me through the crowd, ushered me down the Warwick Road North—a quick stop for two orders of fish'n'chips, grease pouring through the newspapers, Mick's T-shirt by now a work of art—and then across the street into the pub, where, after three quick rounds at the bar, Mick bought a further two pints before sitting down with me at a table. I was the one who asked that we sit. I was starting to bloat.

In Mick, I felt that I had finally met one of "them." At the same time, I felt that perhaps he wasn't the best one of "them" to have met. There were problems. For a start I could see that he was not going to fit easily into my thesis: he was not unemployed or, it seemed, in any way disenfranchised. Instead he appeared to be a perfectly happy, skilled electrician from Blackpool, recently brought in as part of a team rewiring a block of apartments in London. He also had a very large wad of twenty-pound notes stuffed into his trousers: I know this because Mick continued to buy rounds, and the wad never seemed to diminish.

There had to be quite a lot of money if only because Mick had not missed a match in four years. Not one. In fact, Mick said he couldn't imagine how it would be possible to miss one in the future. The future, I pointed out, was quite a long time, and Mick agreed, but, still, it was not a prospect—"Miss Man United?"—that his mind could accommodate comfortably. I didn't know how he had been permitted to leave his building site earlier in the day to catch the train up to Manchester, but I knew that he intended to be back there first thing in the morning. Some time later in the night, after closing time, he would wander down to Manchester Piccadilly and, with cans of lager stuffed into his coat pockets, make his way to the milk train that would get him to London in time for work. I have since wondered what it would be like to have your house rewired by Mick and imagined

that moment—the children just finishing their breakfast, the rush to get them off to school—when the
bell rings and there, with the members of your curious family clustering around the door beside you, is
Mick, recently ejected from the milk train, still sway-
ing, a light fixture in hand.

It was my turn to buy a round, and when I
returned Mick explained to me how the "firm" worked.
He mentioned some of the characters, whose nicknames
were remarkably self-explanatory: Bone Head, Paraffin
Pete, Speedie, Barmy Bernie, One-Eyed Billy, Red (the
communist), and Daft Donald, a fellow of notoriously
limited intelligence who tended to destroy things with
chains. At the time, he was in jail. For that matter, at
one time or another, just about everyone, if not actually in jail, was at least facing a criminal charge or had
recently been tried for one. Mick, who was not of a
violent disposition, had been arrested once, although it
was, he assured me, an unusual occurrence and one
marred by bad timing: the police happened to enter the

pub the moment that Mick, standing astride the unfortunate lad whom he had almost rendered unconscious, had raised a bar stool in the air, poised to bring it crashing down with maximum force and maximum damage. "But I  wasn't actually going to do it," Mick said. There was no chance to argue, because in no time Mick was up again and heading for the bar, saying over his shoulder, "Same again?"

Same again?

I could not see how I would make it to closing time. I got up to go to the loo—my fifth visit—and, hearing a terrible sloshing sound from within, reached out to a chair for support. Mick's thirst appeared unstoppable, or was at least as unstoppable as his stomach was large, and his stomach was very, very large. By the time I returned from the loo, there he was again, approaching the table, two pint glasses in hand. For a moment, the scene appeared to me in duplicate: a watery second Mick and an endless succession of pint glasses in his many hands. I was in trouble. I exhaled deeply. My stomach rolled. Once again, there was another, completely full pint glass. Once again, the froth on top. It was detestable. I stared at it.

Mick gulped.

Most of the supporters, he went on to explain, alcohol having no visible effect, came from either Manchester or London. "The ones from London are known as the Cockney Reds. Gurney is a Cockney Red. He doesn't travel anywhere unless he's on the jib."

Mick was surprised I didn't know what "being on the jib" meant. I was surprised I was able to pronounce the words.

"Being on the jib," Mick continued, with only a half pint now remaining in his glass, "means never spending money. That's always the challenge. You never want to pay for Underground tickets or train tickets or match tickets. In fact, if you're on the jib when you go abroad, you usually come back in profit."

"In profit?"

"Yeah. You know. Money."

Manchester United's firm was known as the ICJ, the International City Jibbers (named after the British Rail commuter service), and Mick proceeded to list the great moments in the ICJ's history—in Valencia and Barcelona during the World Cup when it was in Spain, in France during the qualifying matches for the European championship. Or Luxembourg. That, apparently, was from where Banana Bob returned wearing a fur coat and diamond rings on each of his fingers. Or Germany. That was where he boarded the train back to London with his underpants full of Deutschmarks. Roy Downes was another one. He had just been released from prison in Bulgaria, where he had been caught trying to crack the hotel safe. And there was Sammy. "Sammy is a professional."

"A professional hooligan?"

"No, no. A professional thief."

Sammy, Roy Downes, and Banana Bob were all leaders, or at least that's how Mick described them. I had no idea that there were leaders. It sounded like some kind of tribe. Clearly I would have to meet them. They were the ones to get to. I pursued the subject.

What, I asked Mick innocently, made a leader exactly?

"Doing," Mick said and then paused, clearly refining his thought, "yes, doing the right thing in the right circumstances at the right time."

Ah. "That's not," I offered gently, "a particularly helpful definition."

I asked if there was one principal leader at United, but Mick said, no, there wasn't one leader, which was a problem, but several. "Sammy, Roy, Banana Bob, Robert the Sneak Thief. They all end up competing with each other. And each has his own firm, his own following— with as many as thirty or forty people. Most of the followers are little fifteen- and sixteen-year-olds who are out to prove they can be a 'bob' and will do anything.

They're the most dangerous. They're the ones who start most of the fights. They're like sublieutenants, and they answer only to their own leader. Sammy probably has the most loyal following."

And then Mick stopped, suddenly.

I thought that my questions were making him uncomfortable—leaders? sublieutenants? little armies?—but, no, Mick was looking at my beer, noticing that, while he had finished his pint, my glass was still full, although I had repeatedly brought it to my lips. "You're not much of a drinker, are you?"

It was eleven o'clock at last, and someone was calling "Time" (beautifully, I thought), and I calculated that in addition to an order of fish'n'chips and a thoroughly indigestible cheeseburger I had had two cans of lager and eight pints of bitter. That was a lot, I thought. I had done rather well. But now Mick was telling me that I wasn't much of a drinker. Mick certainly was. He was not keeping track of what he consumed, but I was so impressed that I was. In addition to a newspaper full of fish'n'chips, his *two* cheeseburgers, his *two* meat pies, his *four* bags of bacon-flavored crisps, *and* the Indian take-out order he was about to purchase on his way to the station, Mick had had the following: four cans of Harp lager, a large part of a bottle of Tesco's vodka, and *eighteen* pints of bitter. As the pub closed, Mick bought a further four cans of lager for the train ride home.

It was an expensive business being a football supporter, and I could see that it was important that Mick not miss work in the morning. For although Mick might have talked about being on the jib as if it were the most natural thing in the world, I noticed that he had a return ticket to London and had had a ticket for the match. All in all, he had spent about sixty pounds that evening. He mentioned that the previous Saturday he had spent about the same. He also said that he had spent £155 the day before on a package tour to Turin for the second match with Juventus. That is, between Saturday and Wednesday,

Mick had spent £275 on football. In all likelihood he would spend another fifty or sixty pounds before the following Saturday—£335 in a week, an exceptional week perhaps, but, even so, more than most members of the British population were spending on their monthly mortgages.

WILLIAM TREVOR

Remembering Mr. Pinkerton

 FEW OF US meet now and again, not often these days, in the Gran Paradiso or the Café Pelican. Once it was downstairs at Bianchi's, but like so much of London, Bianchi's isn't there anymore.

We're of an age now, no longer young yet not entirely old, eating less than we did, drinking a bit less too, though not by much. We have the past in common, and by chance were once clients of Mr. Pinkerton, an accountant who was passed among us in the 1960's, recommended as a miracle worker. In the Gran Paradiso or the Café Pelican, we invariably end up talking about Mr. Pinkerton—about his small idiosyncrasies, and the ways in which he was different from accountants we have subsequently known. We touch upon the subject of gluttony, since it was gluttony that destroyed him, or so we have always assumed. We wonder about its nature and the form it takes, and if St. Thomas Aquinas was fair to designate it a sin when more charitably it might perhaps have been called an eating disorder. We recall other instances of its excesses and other gluttons we have encountered.

I remember them at school—useful boys who would consume our plates of pudding or the cold, stale teatime sausage rolls on Sundays, the porridge that otherwise ended up behind the radiators. There was a man I once accompanied on a railway journey who, having dined in the restaurant car and vexedly complained about the quality of the food, ordered the same meal all over again. Most memorably, though, there was Mr. Pinkerton.

He was in his fifties when we knew him, a cheerful, sandy-haired man of 308 pounds, with small eyes that were puffed away to pinpricks by inflations of the surrounding flesh. With a wife whom none of us ever met, or even saw, but imagined to be small and wiry, forever in a kitchen overall, he occupied a terraced house in Wimbledon in southwest London. The marriage was a late blossoming for both of them, being only a few months old when I placed my modest financial affairs in Mr. Pinkerton's hands. This was one of the first facts he revealed to me and I received the impression, as others did later, that the house was Mrs. Pinkerton's, that her possession of it had even played a part in her husband's decision to relinquish his bachelor status.

"Peckish, old chap?" Mr. Pinkerton inquired in the small, ornament-clad dining room in which all business was conducted. Without waiting for a response, he was already maneuvering his bulk around the table, on which piles of blank ledger pages, pencils, erasers, a pencil sharpener, and pen and ink had been laid out. A few minutes later he returned with two plates of sandwiches—beef, ham, pickle and cheese, sardine, tomato, cucumber—the white bread cut thickly, the plates piled high. On all my visits to the dining room, the procedure never varied. There could be no settling down to the account sheets until the sandwiches were fetched, and when the evening ended there were plates of buttery currant scones to see the stomach through the night.

Mr. Pinkerton belonged to an age long before that of the computer; indeed, he could be said to have predated the typewriter, since his accounts were prepared and submitted to the Inland Revenue in tiny, neat handwriting. Jotting down expenses—meals taken away from home, a proportion of heating and lighting, travel abroad and in the United Kingdom for professional purposes—he estimated rather than recorded. Receipts or other evidence of expenditure didn't feature in his calculations.

"About six hundred, old chap? Say seven? Eight?" There was an entry called "Spare Copies," which had something to do with the purchase of one's own books for promotional purposes. So at least Mr. Pinkerton's literary clients assumed; we never asked, simply agreed to the figures proposed. But born among the china shepherds and shepherdesses, the  Highland cattle and flying geese of that small dining room, the term went into the language and to this day appears on accounts annually submitted to various divisions of the British Inland Revenue. "Wife's salary, old chap?" Mr. Pinkerton would inquire, pen poised again, and would suggest an appropriate sum.

Sometimes he visited me rather than I him. He would arrive in the house in the evening, invited to supper because there was hospitality to be returned.

He always came on foot, crossing the two commons
that separated our neighborhood from his, accompanied by a retriever that matched, proportionally, his
own great size, and carrying a stout black stick ("for
protection, old chap"). On the first of these occasions,
when we sat down to eat, he asked for "a couple of
slices of bread" to go with the potatoes, vegetables,
and meat, and throughout the meal the request was
several times repeated. On future occasions my wife
anticipated the demand by placing within his reach a
sliced loaf that he always managed to finish, chomp-
ing his way through it while also consuming whatever else was on offer. "Shouldn't refer to another
client, of course," he would say between mouthfuls,
and then give us details of a case he was conducting
in some northern town, its outcome relevant since he
hoped for the establishing of a precedent. "Tax
inspector up a gum tree," he would confidently predict, a favorite expression that was always accompanied by a gurgle of mirth. "Friendly cunning" was a

favorite also, the weapon of his attack in taxation matters.

By way of further variation as to rendezvous, Mr. Pinkerton occasionally suggested a meeting in a public house, the big, old-fashioned Henekey's in Holborn where, ensconced in a booth, he ate an inordinate number of Scotch eggs and a couple of plates of potato salad. He once told me that these were the only foods he touched in a public house, they being the only barroom dishes that were "safe." I wasn't entirely sure what he meant by that, nor were the clients among whom his gourmandizing eventually became a talking point. We passed on his predilections when, without embarrassment, they were revealed to one or other of us—a particular fondness for a well-roasted parsnip, how he never left the house in Wimbledon without a supply of iced biscuits in his pockets, how he liked to indulge in a midmorning feast of tea and fruitcake, how he had once in someone's presence eaten forty-one sausages.

Gluttony has been numbered among the deadly sins we live with, presumably because it exemplifies an absence of the restraint that dignifies the human condition. Like its six companions, it is at best unattractive. The boys who waded into accumulations of pudding were popular in the dining hall but despised outside it. The two-dinners man in the restaurant car caused revulsion in the features of the waiters. Eyes looked the other way when Mr. Pinkerton reached out for his forty-first sausage.

Even so, in his case we were not censorious. He conducted our affairs with efficiency and was a card as well. We were fond of him because he was mysterious and eccentric, because he enlivened the routine of work he did for us with the fruits of a prodigious memory, storing away matchbox information and sometimes appearing to know us better than we knew ourselves. "August twenty-sixth, 1952. Day you were married, old chap. A Tuesday, if memory serves." He was always right. If you had to cancel a meeting because of a dentist's appointment, the date and time were recorded forever. "Morning of July fourth, old chap. Upper molar, left, dispatched." All of it, for us, was leaven in the weight of figures and assessments and final demands, and none of us guessed that something was the matter. He was a big man; he ate in order to fill that bulky frame. It never occurred to us that his appetite lay fatally at the heart of his existence, like a cruel tumor.

It is only in retrospect that the bloated figure seems lonely, that the passion that ordered its peculiarities seems in some way sinister. It is only in retrospect that we can speculate with clarity on Mr. Pinkerton's downfall, which for me began as an unheeded intimation on a Sunday morning in 1967 when he tried to borrow 500 pounds. The request came out of the blue, on the telephone, and such was my faith in Mr. Pinkerton's respectability and his professional acumen that I said, of course. I did not yet know that a number of his clients had just been touched for similar sums. Some obliged; others more wisely did not.

As the months went by, the loans remained unpaid and, even worse, the Inland Revenue's Final Notices were now being followed by threats of Immediate Court Action or Distraint on Goods. Men with bowler hats even arrived at some of our houses. "Not to worry, old chap" was Mr. Pinkerton's endlessly repeated response, followed by soothing promises that he would, that very day, speak to the relevant inspector, who had by the sound of things got himself up a gum tree.

But this time he didn't tramp round to the local tax office with his dog and his stick and his old black briefcase. Instead, all over London, Mr. Pinkerton's clients  were in trouble, summoned to the revenue courts, reprimanded, investigated, penalized. Mr. Pinkerton's telephone was cut off; he no longer answered letters.

At the behest of a new accountant, I went to see him in Wimbledon one cold winter's morning, hoping to collect some of my papers.

Mr. Pinkerton was in rags. He had been doing the fires, he explained, leading me into the dining room, but there was no sign of anything like that. "Had a burglary, old chap," he said when I asked about my papers, and when I suggested that surely no burglar would steal material as worthless as account sheets, he simply added that he and Mrs. Pinkerton had experienced the misfortune to have had a fire as well. I wanted to ask him what the matter was, why he was talking about events that clearly hadn't occurred, but somewhere in his small eyes there was a warning that this was private territory, so I desisted.

I never saw him again, but from time to time a fragmentary record of his subsequent career was passed about, downstairs in Bianchi's in those days. The house in Wimbledon was seized by a mortgage company; he was struck off as an accountant; he and Mrs. Pinkerton were in pauper's lodgings. There was a theory that he had destroyed all the papers in his care—a form of symbolic suicide—and a year or so later death was there for real—he died in the streets one day.

Our speculations mourn him. "Peckish, old chap?" comes the echo from his heyday, the question asked of himself after dinner with a client. Tins of peas and beans and meatballs, beetroot in vinegar, cold apple dumpling are laid out to see the stomach through the night. And later on, in dreams, his table's spread again, with meats and soups and celery in parsley sauce, with cauliflower and leeks and roasted parsnips, potatoes mashed and fried, crème brûlée, crème caramel, meringues and brandy snaps, mints and Turkish delight.

If some, we wonder, are selected to be the recipients of the gifts that lift humanity to its heights, can it be said that the others are chosen to bear the burdens by which some balance may be struck? And we wonder if the gluttony we knew was a form of disguise or compensation for an inner emptiness, if the burden that is called a sin was more complicated than it seemed to be. We mull uncertainly over that, although we knew the man quite well, and in the end we leave the question unresolved, as somehow it seems meant to be. Blue-suited and courteous, the stout accountant went gracefully to the grave. In the Gran Paradiso or the Café Pelican, with his ghost among us, he hints at that.

AUTHOR BIOGRAPHIES

In addition to his work in movies as a screenwriter, director, and actor, WOODY ALLEN (born Allen Stewart Konigsberg in 1935 in Brooklyn, New York) has written several books, including *Without Feathers, Side Effects,* and *Getting Even,* from which "Notes from the Overfed" is taken.

The ANONYMOUS "Moderation in Food" is taken from a singularly smug 18th-century tract.

RUSSELL BAKER is a Pulitzer Prize-winning author of a dozen books, including *Growing Up* and *The Good Times,* as well as a longtime columnist and humorist for the *New York Times,* in which "Francs and Beans" first appeared.

BILL BUFORD, who for nearly twenty years has edited the literary magazine *Granta,* spent time in the 1980s venturing to various cities in Europe with English soccer fans. The resulting book, *Among the Thugs,* chronicled the mayhem that the author witnessed and partook in.

A journalist, essayist, and one of the most insightful in a long line of British commentators on the American scene, HENRY FAIRLIE authored several books on the United States and its politics, including *The Kennedy Promise* and *The Spoiled Child of the Western World.*

"I'm a reporter," she once said. "I write about the basic things in life— and one of them is eating." Through 25 books, including *The Gastronomical Me, How to Cook a Wolf,* and *The Art of Eating,* M.F.K. FISHER wrote about the basic things in life—food, hunger, travel, friends—with a reporter's eye and a poet's heart.

BEN JONSON was one of England's greatest playwrights as well as an influential poet, whose first original play, *Every Man in His Humour,* was staged with William Shakespeare as a member of the cast.

Despite a relatively slim body of work, the literary world's doyenne of laziness, FRAN LEBOWITZ, would be included in just about any list of America's funniest writers, even if she never wrote another line as long as she lives . . . a distinct possibility.

DIANE MASON didn't start writing "seriously" until she was 31. She now has more than a dozen published stories to her credit, and is working on her first novel. Her children feel neglected.

Arbiter Elegantum ("judge of elegance") at the court of Nero, PETRONIUS is the suspected author of *The Satyricon*, an unusually vivid portrayal of court life in Imperial Rome.

Though JOHN POWERS has resolved to commit all seven deadly sins by age 50, he has not yet managed to progress beyond lust, sloth and gluttony. Powers intends to endow the Jack Falstaff chair of gastroenterology at Harvard, where he survived for four years on meatball sandwiches and whiskey sours.

The great English dramatist WILLIAM SHAKESPEARE penned his masterpiece, *King Henry the Fourth*, in 1599.

JOHN KENNEDY TOOLE's comic masterpiece, *A Confederacy of Dunces*, is the stuff of publishing legend: a bereaved mother presses her dead son's manuscript on a reluctant, famous author; author relents, reads, is amazed; book is published; rave reviews ensue; a posthumous Pulitzer is awarded in 1981. John Kennedy Toole committed suicide at 31.

WILLIAM TREVOR is the author of eighteen books, including short story collections and novels. He has won *The Hudson Review*'s Bennett Award, and has twice received the Whitbread Prize for Fiction.

ACKNOWLEDGEMENTS

"Notes from the Overfed" from *Getting Even* by Woody Allen ©1971 by Woody Allen, reprinted by permission of Vintage Books, a division of Random House, Inc.

"Francs and Beans" from *So This is Depravity* by Russell Baker ©1980 by Russell Baker, reprinted by permission of St. Martin's Press, New York, NY.

Excerpt from *Among the Thugs* by Bill Buford ©1991, 1990 by William Buford. Reprinted by permission of W.W. Norton & Company, Inc.

"Gluttony or Gula" by Henry Fairlie reprinted by permission of *The New Republic*.

"G is for Gluttony" reprinted with permission of Macmillan General Reference, USA, a division of Simon & Schuster, Inc. from *The Art of Eating* by M.F.K. Fisher ©1949 by M.F.K. Fisher. Copyright renewed ©1976 by Mary Kennedy Friede.

"The Fran Lebowitz High Stress Diet and Exercise Program" from *The Fran Lebowitz Reader* by Fran Lebowitz ©1971 by Fran Lebowitz, reprinted by permission of Vintage Books, a division of Random House, Inc.

"Feast" by Diane Mason reprinted by permission of the author.

"Sinfully Good" by John Powers reprinted by permission of *The Boston Globe*.

Excerpt from *A Confederacy of Dunces* ©1980 by Thelma D. Toole. Reprinted by permission of Louisiana State University.

"Remembering Mr. Pinkerton" by William Trevor ©1993 by The New York Times Company. Reprinted by permission.